Disney
The
ARISTOCATS

Ladybird

In the beautiful city of Paris, there once lived a wealthy old lady called Madame Bonfamille. Her home was an elegant mansion on a tree-lined avenue. She enjoyed music and art… but more than anything else, Madame Bonfamille loved her cats.

There was Duchess, a beautiful white cat, and her three adorable kittens Berlioz, Toulouse and Marie. They ate the very best food from their own special trays, and slept in their very own canopied basket. And there were lots of wonderful things to play with – like the grand piano, a gramophone and balls of fluffy wool.

For these were no ordinary cats… they were *Aristocats!*

Early each morning Madame Bonfamille would ride through the park with her Aristocats. And on their return the three little kittens would take up their lessons.

Marie practised her singing, because she hoped one day to be an opera singer. Berlioz played the piano and Toulouse liked to paint. He painted the floor, the table, his paws, in fact, everywhere!

Madame Bonfamille would proudly watch each kitten in turn, with Duchess smiling at her side. "You are all artists, my treasures," Madame would say.

The cats also had another, but most unusual, friend – Roquefort the mouse. He lived in a hole in the kitchen wall, and would often come to dip his biscuits in the kittens' milk. He knew he would come to no harm at all in this house. For Aristocats would never chase mice, or scratch or hiss.

Madame's oldest friend was her lawyer Monsieur Georges Hautecourt. He was ninety years old, but still loved to speed across the city in his open-topped car.

One day Madame Bonfamille decided to phone her friend – it was time to make a will. She wanted to be certain that the Aristocats would always enjoy the good life, even if she were no longer there.

A few minutes later Monsieur Hautecourt arrived and the butler helped him up the stairs.

When the butler had gone, and all the lawyer's papers were spread out on the table, Madame Bonfamille began, "I wish to leave my entire fortune to Duchess and the kittens. While they live, my faithful butler Edgar will take care of them. And at the end of their lives, the remaining fortune will be his."

Downstairs, unknown to his mistress, Edgar the butler had heard every word through the speaking tube. And the more he thought about the will, the angrier he became. For Edgar had always secretly hated Madame's pets.

"Hmmph!" he grumbled to himself. "Cats inherit first, and I come after them. Oh, it's not fair. Anyway, since every cat has nine lives, I don't stand a chance of getting anything – they could live far longer than me! No! They'll have to go. Then *everything* will be mine!"

As Edgar started to prepare supper for the kittens, an evil thought developed in his mind.

"Ah, good evening, my little ones," said Edgar, as the Aristocats bounded towards him at supper time. "Here is your favourite dish, prepared in a very special way. It's called crême de la crême à la Edgar." And, closing the door behind him, he added, "Sleep well!"

In the kitchen, everything went quiet except for the sound of four lapping tongues. Or rather five, for Roquefort had joined them for supper, as usual.

"Mmmm! Delicious!" he said, licking his lips. "This calls for another biscuit. I'll be right back."

But Roquefort had hardly reached his hole before he fell into a deep sleep, and Duchess and the kittens soon snuggled down in their basket.

When Edgar was certain that all of the cats were asleep, he went back into the kitchen and picked up the basket. Noiselessly he entered the garage, strapped the basket to his motor bike and sped away into the countryside. He intended to drown the cats in the first river he came to.

But, luckily, two farm dogs spoiled his plans. They rushed out at him as he travelled down the road. Edgar panicked and the basket fell gently to the ground. For fear of being bitten, he didn't dare turn back for the basket or stop until he had arrived safely at Madame's mansion.

At sunrise Duchess yawned and put her head out of the basket. "Oh!" she cried. "Where am I? I'm not at home at all." Then realising that she must remain brave in front of the kittens, she looked around to see what could be done.

Suddenly she noticed a handsome alley cat walking towards her. He was singing to himself, "I'm Abraham Delacey… Giuseppe Casey… Thomas O'Malley… O'Malley the alley cat."

Duchess decided she could trust him and, introducing herself and the kittens, she asked if he could direct them to Paris.

O'Malley gallantly offered to take them there himself.

It was a long way back to the city and O'Malley knew that the kittens would not be strong enough to walk all the way, so he told them to jump inside a milk lorry on its way to the station.

From there they followed the railway track on and on, until it crossed the river. "Now do be careful, children," warned Duchess, as a train whistled towards them. "Move to the side and hold on tight!"

But she was too late. As the train gusted by them, Marie lost her balance and fell into the river below.

O'Malley didn't waste a second. He dived to the rescue and, holding Marie in his mouth, scrambled towards the river bank. The little kitten was safe… but it would be many hours before they were home and dry.

As evening fell they reached the edge of the city. But the kittens could go no further.

"Listen, Duchess," said O'Malley, "it's late and the kittens can hardly stand up. My home isn't far from here. It's nothing special, but it's peaceful and quiet."

He led the short way across the rooftops, and soon they could hear a band playing jazz music. "Oh no!" cried O'Malley. "That sounds like Scat Cat and his gang. Perhaps we'd better look for somewhere else."

"Oh no!" said Duchess, smiling. "I'd like to see your home… *and* meet Scat Cat and his gang!"

They looked down through the nearest skylight and watched the alley cat band in full swing.

As soon as the kittens heard the music, they forgot their tiredness and joined in with the band. Berlioz helped the Siamese on the piano. Toulouse and Scat Cat blew the trumpets and Marie sang along at the top of her voice. Duchess and O'Malley danced until midnight, and only just remembered to put the kittens to bed!

It was a lovely night and, as the moon shone brightly above them, Duchess and O'Malley sat talking on a nearby chimney. "Thomas," she said, "your friends are delightful. And thank you for offering us your home. You were there just when we needed you."

"From now on, this can be your home," said Thomas, staring lovingly into Duchess's big blue eyes.

But Duchess knew how much Madame would be missing them, and so she sadly refused.

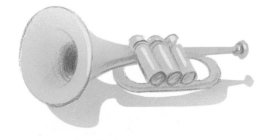

Duchess and the kittens ran straight into Edgar's trap. He bundled them away at once into a trunk in the barn. Then he raced back inside to order a delivery van… to take a large package to Timbuktu!

As Edgar made his phone call, Roquefort, who'd watched everything, rushed over to the trunk. "Duchess, kittens, are you all right?"

"Yes! But please hurry," answered Duchess. "Go and find O'Malley. He's the only one who can help us, and he can't have gone far."

It had started to rain, but Roquefort ran as quickly as he could. He managed to catch up with O'Malley at the next corner.

"I'm going to need help," shouted O'Malley. "You go get Scat and his gang. I'll go ahead. Don't worry – just mention my name."

As he made his way down the alley, poor Roquefort was not so sure. "Well, that's easy for… *what's his name* to say. He's got nine lives. I've only got one."

Suddenly he was caught up by his tail and saw in front of him a huge pair of cat's eyes. "Well! What's a little swinger like you doing on our side of town?" asked the Siamese.

"Oh please!" cried Roquefort. "I was sent here for help – by a cat."

"Really, how interesting!" mocked the Siamese, bringing out his claws. The rest of the gang started laughing.

"No, honest! He told me just to mention his name. It was O'… O'Brien," stuttered Roquefort, terrified. "It was O'Grady… No… Wait!… Oh, why did I listen to that O'Malley cat?"

No sooner had Roquefort said these words than the alley cats raced at once to the rescue.

Back at the barn, Edgar was chasing O'Malley round with a pitchfork and eventually pinned him against the wall. But not for long! Scat Cat and his friends burst in, and spitting and scratching, the whole jazz band attacked the butler.

Roquefort worked out how to unlock the padlock, and O'Malley helped Duchess and her family to climb out of the trunk.

Edgar tried his best to stop them, but he tripped… and fell head first into the trunk. O'Malley slammed the lid down firmly.

Soon a delivery van arrived, and the cats watched happily as the driver took the trunk away.

Madame Bonfamille never did work out why Edgar had left so quickly. "I'm sure, if Edgar had known about the will, he would have stayed here," she said. "But it is wonderful to have you all back.

"And I think this young man is very handsome," she added, combing O'Malley's fur. "Shall we keep him in the family? Now, smile and say cheese!"

"Did someone say cheese?" asked Roquefort, running to watch the family photograph.

Later Madame Bonfamille changed her will again – to include O'Malley and to start up a home for all the alley cats of Paris. And, of course, they all lived happily ever after.

Ladybird books are widely available, but in case of difficulty may be ordered by post or telephone from:
Ladybird Books – Cash Sales Department Littlegate Road Paignton Devon TQ3 3BE Telephone 0803 554761

A catalogue record for this book is available from the British Library

Published by Ladybird Books Ltd Loughborough Leicestershire UK
LADYBIRD and the device of a Ladybird are trademarks of Ladybird Books Ltd